# This book belongs to

_____

**tate publishing**
CHILDREN'S DIVISION

Published by Tate Publishing & Enterprises, LLC
127 E. Trade Center Terrace | Mustang, Oklahoma 73064 USA
1.888.361.9473 | www.tatepublishing.com

Tate Publishing is committed to excellence in the publishing industry. The company reflects the philosophy established by the founders, based on Psalm 68:11,
*"The Lord gave the word and great was the company of those who published it."*

Book design copyright © 2012 by Tate Publishing, LLC. All rights reserved.
*Cover and interior design by Blake Brasor*
*Illustrations by Katie Brooks*

Published in the United States of America

ISBN: 978-1-62024-493-7
1. Juvenile Fiction / General
2. Juvenile Fiction / Fairy Tales & Folklore / General
12.08.02

# Leppy and the Magic Pot

## by Lauren Schoenbauer

# Dedication

Dedicated to my grandma, Sue Mordan, and my mom,
Lynn Schoenbauer, for keeping Leppy alive.

# Preface

This story was inspired by a game I used to play as a child. My siblings and I would put leaves into a pot, say magic words, and leave the room.

When we returned after a few minutes, we looked into the pot to find that the leaves had been replaced with candy! I think it only began because my grandma wanted a break from my mom and her siblings. But my mom passed down the tradition to me and my brothers and sisters, just like in this story. Every time we played, we were thrilled at the outcome. I truly believed there was a leprechaun that lived in our house! I've included a picture of the Magic Pot that caused so many exciting moments in my childhood.

Also pictured is a leprechaun that has always sat on the clock in our basement—our only idea of what Leppy might look like since we've never actually seen him.

In spring the leprechauns were busier than ever.
It was time they began their annual endeavor.
After storms in the spring, there's often a rainbow.
The leprechauns made coins to fill the pot below.

The work began when the snow was all gone,
The leprechauns labored from dusk until dawn.
They filled endless pots with all of their gold
For a few lucky people to one day behold.

From the outside Leppy seemed to fit in
With fire-red hair on his head and his chin.
He wore tall socks, green pants, and a vest,
The way leprechauns look at their best.

Each one had the skills; they knew how to work fast.
But poor little Leppy was always done last.
As much as he tried to succeed like the rest,
Leppy's hard work was never the best.

When he tried to work fast, his coins became lumpy.
Instead of smooth gold, the surface was bumpy.
The others would laugh at his misshapen work.
Leppy's mistakes made the leprechauns smirk.

Everyone noticed how few coins he made.
He brushed off their jokes, but his spirit did fade.
*This job making coins just isn't for me,*
*I need something new,* thought little Leppy.

So that night he left home and took all that he had.
With his top hat and green clothes he was clad.
He didn't have a plan, but the direction felt right.
He walked through the day and all through the night.

After wandering far, he needed some rest,
So he gathered up leaves and made a small nest.
While he lay there asleep, he dreamed a great dream,
He saw a small house that sat by a stream.

He awoke with a start and set off on his way
To follow his dream on that fine spring day.
He didn't walk far, 'cause soon he could see
The place he knew he was meant to be.

Leppy's long voyage ended up at a house.
Quite a long journey when you're small as a mouse.
He was meant to be here, he just didn't know why.
*Who wants a leprechaun?* he thought with a sigh.

He saw through the window the shadow of a child.
At this his thoughts began running wild.
Then she looked out, and Leppy froze on the lawn.
What would she think of a wee leprechaun?

But it was there that they met, best friends from the start.
From that day on they were never far apart.
They swam in the lake and gazed at the stars
And pretended to be like creatures from Mars.

They giggled all day and read books late at night
Under the covers with a flashlight.
The wall was covered in pictures they'd drawn,
And they made special forts out on the lawn.

*Leppy is my secret*, the little girl thought,
So together they invented the perfect hiding spot.
A pile of soft leaves in a pot that was shiny,
A perfect home for someone so tiny.
She brought it to her room, set it on the floor,
And hid it in the corner right behind the door.

Leppy stayed  in the pot when she was away
And invented new games for the buddies to play.
One day before school the two friends made a plan,
And that was when the game "Magic Pot" began.
The girl put fresh leaves in Leppy's special pot
Just what he needed to make a sleeping spot.
When Leppy took the gifts he left a surprise.
This first time was candy in the "fun size."

Other times he left juicy gumdrops
Or swirly, twirly lollipops.
He'd leave chocolate chips, tiny and sweet.
Leppy's "thank you gifts" were always a treat.

The girl kept him a secret, never told anyone,
About her small friend and all of their fun.
Until one rainy day when there was nothing to do
She and her mom decided to make some hot stew.
Leppy knew it was time for the world to know his name
And share leprechaun joy with this new game.
Her mom found a pot and added bay leaves and spice,
The kinds that make the whole room smell nice.
As they turned away Leppy scurried to the pot.
He gathered up leaves and put chocolate in their spot.

The girl turned around and was filled with glee
When she saw the treats from little Leppy.

"Leppy!" she cried, but by then he was gone.
You have to be quick to catch a leprechaun.
"Who's Leppy?" asked her mother, utterly confused
And noticing the girl was suddenly amused.
She shared her story about her little green friend,
And the leaves she would give and the treats he would send.

Then they both gave Leppy leaves for his bed
In the small shiny pot where he rested his head.
And just like in their game, he left a surprise,
Once again it was candy in the "fun size."

Magic Pot still works today; it's a leprechaun's game.
Put leaves in a pot and call Leppy's name.
"Shimboree, shimborah, Leppy come please!"
Say the magic words over a pot full of leaves.

You mustn't be watching or Leppy won't play.
He only appears after you've gone away.
Now Leppy needs you to play Magic Pot,
Just leaves and love, but don't make it hot!

Try it one day, no matter where you're from.
Put some leaves in a pot, and your Leppy might come.

 LIVE

# listen|imagine|view|experience

## AUDIO BOOK DOWNLOAD INCLUDED WITH THIS BOOK!

In your hands you hold a complete digital entertainment package. Besides purchasing the paper version of this book, this book includes a free download of the audio version of this book. Simply use the code listed below when visiting our website. Once downloaded to your computer, you can listen to the book through your computer's speakers, burn it to an audio CD or save the file to your portable music device (such as Apple's popular iPod) and listen on the go!

How to get your free audio book digital download:

1. Visit www.tatepublishing.com and click on the e|LIVE logo on the home page.
2. Enter the following coupon code:
   72e3-2d30-b229-e0a4-5197-866d-9ca2-7838
3. Download the audio book from your e|LIVE digital locker and begin enjoying your new digital entertainment package today!